The Mouse Who Owned the Sun

The Mouse Who Owned the Sun

by Sally Derby • *Illustrations by* Friso Henstra

Four Winds Press ✳ *New York*
Maxwell Macmillan Canada   *Toronto*
Maxwell Macmillan International
New York   Oxford   Singapore   Sydney

SUNSET CASTLE

SEED PLENTIFUL VILLAGE

Four Winds Press, Macmillan Publishing Company, 866 Third Avenue, New York, NY 10022   Maxwell Macmillan Canada, Inc., 1200 Eglinton Avenue East, Suite 200, Don Mills, Ontario M3C 3N1 Macmillan Publishing Company is part of the Maxwell Communication Group of Companies.   First edition   Printed and bound in Singapore   10 9 8 7 6 5 4 3 2 1   The text of this book is set in Galliard. The illustrations are rendered in pen and ink and watercolor. Library of Congress Cataloging-in-Publication Data   Derby, Sally.   The mouse who owned the sun / by Sally Derby ; illustrations by Friso Henstra. — 1st ed.   p.   cm.   Summary: A little mouse learns that there is much more to the world than he'd ever imagined.   ISBN 0-02-766965-3 [1. Mice—Fiction.]   I. Henstra, Friso, ill.   II. Title.   PZ7.D44175Mo 1993 [E]—dc20   91-40965

To my mother, who would have loved *this* mouse
—S.D.

To Piet
—F.H.

SUNFLOWER FIELD

DEEP, DEEP WOODS

MOUSE HOLLOW

KINGFISHER BOG

N

Once there was a mouse who thought he owned the sun. Every morning he woke while it was still dark. Lying in bed, he would say, "I feel like getting up now. Okay, Sun, it's time to rise." And sure enough, very soon the sun would rise.

Late in the day, when the shadows were lengthening, he would close his door, tuck himself into bed, and say sleepily, "I do believe I'm getting tired. You'd better set, Sun." And every night, shortly after that, the sun would go down.

The little mouse lived all alone at the foot of a big oak in a deep, deep woods. One day, just as he finished his lunch and began brushing the crumbs off his tablecloth, he heard a knock on the door. He smoothed his whiskers, straightened his suspenders, and went to answer it.

"Good day," he said, looking with surprise at the pretty young mouse dressed for hiking who stood on his doorstep.

"Good day," she answered. "I wonder if you would be so kind as to tell me where I am? I seem to have lost my way."

The little mouse said importantly, "I'm happy to help. You're in the Deep, Deep Woods."

"But in what part of the Deep, Deep Woods?" the hiker asked. "Am I in the northern part, approaching the Sunflower Field, or over to the east, near Kingfisher Bog?"

Kingfisher Bog? The Sunflower Field? The little mouse had never heard of either one. "I'm afraid I don't know," he answered, not feeling at all important now. "You see, I have never ventured very far from my little house."

"Then you have missed some splendid times," the pretty young mouse said with a smile. "I love to go exploring. Why don't you try it sometime? If you do, and you find yourself near the Sunflower Field, stop to see me. The village I live in, Seed Plentiful, is snuggled into the bank at the edge of the field, and my house is the last one on the lane that leads into the Deep, Deep Woods. But now I must be on my way." And with a friendly wave, the hiker hurried across the little mouse's front yard and disappeared into the trees.

The little mouse went back into his house. "How embarrassing!" he said aloud. "As owner of the sun, I really should be more knowledgeable. Tomorrow I will go exploring."

Early next morning he wrapped a cheese in a red bandanna,
tied the bandanna to a stick, hoisted the stick over his shoulder,
and set off.

By and by he found a little path. He followed the path till it
joined a road that led to the edge of the forest. The little mouse
stood at the forest's edge and saw that the road wandered across

a grassy plain. "My," he said, "the world is even bigger than I thought. It's a good thing I brought a lunch."

He had started down the road, whistling a jaunty tune, when he heard a loud sound. In a cloud of dust, a troop of soldiers on horseback came galloping along. One horse came so close the little mouse had to dodge out of the way. He was frightened for a minute, and being frightened made him angry.

"Stop!" he bellowed.

The startled soldiers reined in their horses, and their captain called out, "Who orders the King's Guard to stop?"

"I do!" said the little mouse, stepping back into the road and brushing off his jacket. "You almost ran over me. And if you'd done that, who would tell the sun to come up tomorrow?"

"Why, it's just a little mouse," laughed the Captain. "A tiny little mouse with a great big voice."

The little mouse frowned. "I may be little, but I own the sun. I tell the sun when to rise and when to set, and if you don't treat me more respectfully, I'll have to tell it to teach you a lesson."

"Tell the sun? No one tells the sun what to do."

The soldiers moved uneasily on their horses. They hoped their captain wasn't making the wrong mouse angry.

"Just watch!" said the little mouse. He puffed out his chest, took a deep breath, and pointed his pink nose up at the sun. "Sun!" he cried. "This man thinks you won't obey me. Hide your face from him!"

Now, as luck would have it, at that exact moment a wind sprang up and blew a storm cloud across the face of the sun. The rest of the sky was clear and blue, but that big black cloud hid the sun from sight.

"Now I guess you believe me," said the little mouse. "You're lucky I didn't tell the sun to come down and burn you." And he started off, his tail held high.

"Wait!" called the Captain. "I see you really do own the sun!" The little mouse slowed down, and the Captain urged his horse forward. "If you please, Sir, our king will be angry if we tell him we didn't invite the owner of the sun to visit the palace. Won't you come to meet the King?"

Now that the Captain was showing some manners, he wasn't such a bad fellow, the little mouse thought. "Is it far to where the King lives?" he asked.

"Not far at all," said the Captain. He dismounted from his horse and took a map from his pocket. Then he unfolded the map and spread it on the ground. "This is where we are," he pointed. He moved his finger to a picture of a castle. "And this is Sunset Castle, where the King lives."

The little mouse had never seen a map before, and this was a beautiful map with curving lines, bright colors, and many intriguing names. Trees painted in a rich, dark green marked the location of the Deep, Deep Woods. The little mouse looked closely. In a clear space near the edge of the woods he saw the words MOUSE HOLLOW printed in bright red letters. His whiskers twitched with curiosity. There certainly was a lot to the rest of the world! And how he longed to see what kind of place Mouse Hollow might be!

"I don't think I'll have time to go see the King," the little mouse said. "The world is much bigger than I thought. I brought only enough food for lunch, so I need to be back home at suppertime."

"If you'll ride with me, Sir," said the Captain, "it won't take long."

"Well, I guess I can spare an hour or so," said the little mouse. The Captain set him on the saddle, then mounted the horse himself.

"Forward!" he shouted to his men, and off they all went.

It was a little past noon when they came to the gates of a castle. The Captain called to the gatekeeper, "An important visitor to see the King! Let us pass!"

As he rode through the gates, the little mouse looked around with wonder. "This is a very large castle," he thought. "So the king who lives here must be very important. But not as important as I," he reminded himself. "After all, lots of kings own castles, but only *I* own the sun."

"I'm sure the King will want to see you right away, Sir," said the Captain, setting the little mouse lightly on the ground.

"That's nice of him," said the little mouse, "but he'll have to wait a bit. It's time for me to eat my lunch." He undid his bandanna and spread it on the ground. Then, picking up the cheese, he said graciously, "It's a good-sized cheese. Would you care for a little?"

The soldiers could see there was really only a mouse-sized portion, so they declined politely. They sat down in a circle to wait.

"If you please, Sir," said the Captain, when the mouse was finished, "the King isn't fond of overcast days. Would you mind making the sun come back out?"

"Not at all," said the little mouse, wiping his whiskers with his handkerchief. He looked up. "You can come out now, Sun!" he cried. Nothing happened. "Don't keep me waiting!" the mouse called sternly. The wind began to pick up, and the edge of the cloud lightened, but still no sun. The little mouse stood up and stamped his foot. "I said, '*Now*!'" he shouted in his biggest voice.

And just then (Oh, lucky little mouse!), the sun peeped through the cloud. "That's better," said the little mouse. "All right, now we can go see the King."

Now, while the little mouse had been eating, some of the soldiers had hurried to tell the King about him. They whispered that he was a powerful mouse with a voice like thunder, who could cause the sun to appear and disappear fifty times in one hour, who could burn down the castle if he wanted.

Therefore, when the little mouse knocked on the throne-room door, the King opened it himself, just to be extra-polite. "Welcome, O Mighty One," the King said. "Won't you come in?"

"Thank you," said the little mouse.

The King put a small cushion on the floor in front of the throne, and the little mouse climbed up on it. Then he and the King both sat down.

The King asked, "Does the sun really do whatever you say?"

"Don't you believe it?" asked the little mouse.

"Oh, I believe it," said the King, who had no wish to make the little mouse angry. "But if you wouldn't mind, I would like to see a small demonstration. You might tell the sun to set, for example."

"But if the sun sets now," the little mouse said, "it will be night, and I will have to find my way home in the dark. I shouldn't like that."

"Well," said the King, "as soon as the sun sets, you can tell it to rise again."

The little mouse gazed kindly at the King. "Now, think, Your Majesty," he said. "If I tell the sun to set, it will go down in the west. And then it will have to travel all the way around this big world to get over to the east, where it rises. I'd have to wait a long time before I could tell it to rise again."

"I see the problem," said the King. "Tell me, then, how long have you owned the sun?"

"All my life," answered the little mouse.

"I don't think that's fair," the King said. "You should let somebody else have a turn."

The little mouse looked surprised. "I suppose you have a point," he said.

"I'll tell you what," said the King. "How about selling it to me?"

"Sell the sun?" the little mouse asked.

"I'll give you whatever you like," offered the King. "Gold. Emeralds. Rubies. Your own palace."

The little mouse laughed. "What would I do with gold or emeralds or rubies? And as for my own palace, I'm happy with my little house in the woods. But," he added, "there is one thing you could give me in exchange for the sun."

"Name it!" said the King.

"I should like a map like your captain has," said the little mouse. "It seems there is much more to this world than I had thought. I will need a map if I am to see it properly. Then I can go exploring and mark my journeys in dotted lines on the map and put circles around the places I visit."

"Done!" cried the King, and he and the little mouse went back into the courtyard. There the little mouse stopped and looked up at the sky.

"Sun! Oh, Sun!" he called. "I have exchanged you for a wonderful map of the world. I want to thank you for all the years you have been obedient to me, and introduce you to your new master, the King."

Then, turning to the King, he said, "Now, listen to me carefully, Your Majesty. You must learn to wake very early in the morning, so that you can be up in time to tell the sun to rise. And you must always be in your bed when the shadows lengthen late in the day so that you can tell the sun to set before he gets too weary."

"I will do exactly as you say," promised the King. "Have a safe trip home, and I wish you many happy journeys."

The little mouse and the Captain rode off down the road. When they reached the point where the road branched off into the forest, the Captain stopped his horse and drew the wonderful map from his pocket. "Well, good-bye," said the Captain.

"Good-bye," said the little mouse. "Ride carefully."

Going back home, he compared his path with the markings on the map and was excited to find that his way led in the same direction as Mouse Hollow. He came nearer and nearer—past this curiously shaped rock, past that crooked tree—till, just as he arrived at the spot the map called Mouse Hollow, he found himself at his own front door!

"So this is Mouse Hollow!" he marveled. "To think all along my home had a name, and I didn't even know! I believe in the morning I'll put a sign out front. Then if someone else is lost in the woods, he will see my sign and look at his map and know right where he is. The world is even bigger than I thought, but there is company closer than I realized.

"It has been an interesting day," he continued as he opened his door, "and I have learned a great deal about the world, but it is good to be home again."

He fixed himself a bite of supper, then took off his jacket, shook the dust from it, and hung it on a peg on the wall. He brushed his teeth, put on his pajamas, and climbed into bed. As he lay there, planning where to hang his map, and when to begin his journey to the Sunflower Field and Seed Plentiful, his eyes began to get heavy and he found himself yawning.

"I hope the King remembers to tell the sun to set soon," he thought, "for I am getting sleepy."

And the King must have remembered, for in a few minutes the sun set, and the stars came out, and the tired little mouse fell fast asleep.